ROLLO'S MANY COATS

by REED DUNCAN
illustrated by KEITH FRAWLEY

ABOUT THE AUTHOR:

Reed Duncan is an author as well as a former
reading instructor, teacher, and school administrator.
He lives in Vermont. The Rollo stories are based on
Reed and his real-life, rambunctious bulldog,
who has many, many coats.

PENGUIN WORKSHOP
An Imprint of Penguin Random House LLC, New York

Penguin supports copyright. Copyright fuels creativity, encourages diverse voices,
promotes free speech, and creates a vibrant culture. Thank you for buying an authorized edition
of this book and for complying with copyright laws by not reproducing, scanning, or distributing
any part of it in any form without permission. You are supporting writers and allowing
Penguin to continue to publish books for every reader.

Text copyright © 2020 by Reed Duncan. Illustrations copyright © 2020
by Penguin Random House LLC. All rights reserved. First published in hardcover in 2020
by Penguin Workshop. This paperback edition published in 2021 by Penguin Workshop,
an imprint of Penguin Random House LLC, New York. PENGUIN and PENGUIN WORKSHOP
are trademarks of Penguin Books Ltd, and the W colophon is
a registered trademark of Penguin Random House LLC.
Manufactured in China.

Visit us online at www.penguinrandomhouse.com.

Library of Congress Control Number: 2020939136

ISBN 9781524792503   10 9 8 7 6 5 4 3 2 1

ROLLO'S MANY COATS

by REED DUNCAN
illustrated by KEITH FRAWLEY

PENGUIN WORKSHOP

Rollo, are you ready for the party tonight?
We need to find your party coat.

You have all kinds of coats,
but only ONE party coat.

Let's look for it!

No, not that coat, Rollo.

That's a winter coat for when it is cold.
It's too heavy for a party.

Let's keep looking.

No, not that one, Rollo.

Your raincoat is for wet days.

No, not that coat, Rollo.

The furry coat is too fancy.
It is not the coat we are looking for.

No, Rollo.

Your checkered coat is a special coat,
but it is not your party coat.

No, not that coat, Rollo.
That's the hiding coat.

Will we ever find your party coat?

Let's keep looking.

No, we're not looking for your vest, Rollo.

It has no sleeves.
It is not a coat.

No, Rollo, we're not looking for
the walking coat,

or the reading coat,

or the eating coat.

None of these are your party coat.

Let's keep looking!

The pocket coat with all the pouches?

No. That is not the party coat, either.

The dancing coat means that
it is time to go dancing!

But tonight's party is not a dancing party.

That is not the right coat, either.

Ah-ha! Yes!

Rollo, we found your party coat!

Do you know what kind of party
it will be tonight?

A birthday party!

Happy birthday, Rollo!